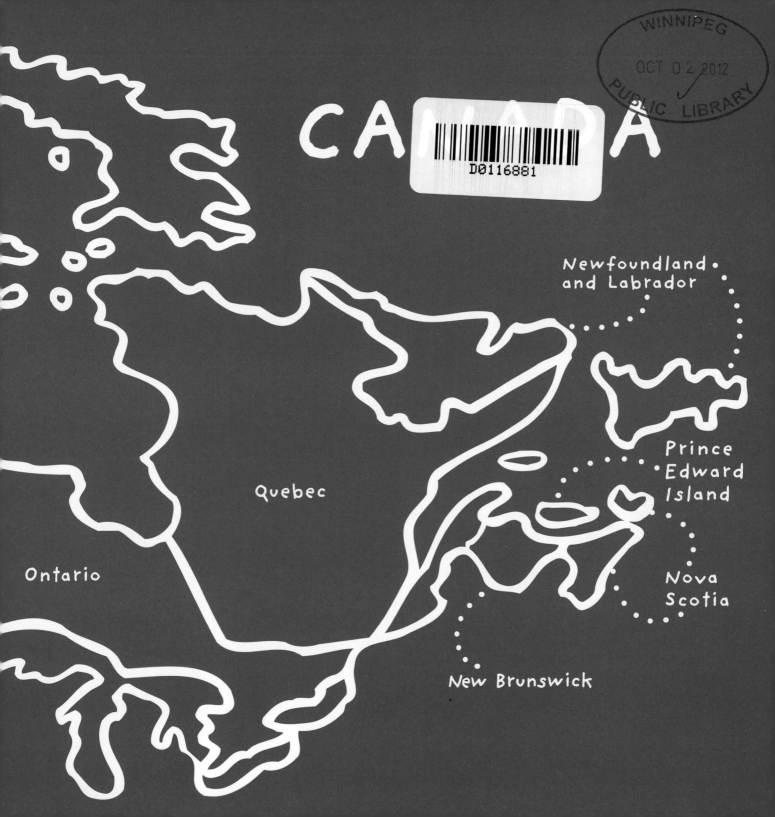

CANADA

Newfoundland
and Labrador

Prince
Edward
Island

Nova
Scotia

Quebec

Ontario

New Brunswick

Canada
in Words

Per-Henrik Gürth

Kids Can Press

beaver

canoe

totem pole

grizzly

maple syrup

sugar shack

ice fishing

toque

long johns

snow shoes

lobster

schooner

hockey

Stanley Cup

polar bear

inukshuk

log cabin

blueberries

lacrosse

maple leaf

lakes

loon

poutine

toboggan

prairies

mounties

mountains

salmon

bush plane

northern
lights

For Ruth Charisius

Kids Can Press acknowledges the financial support of the Government of Ontario, through the Ontario Media Development Corporation's Ontario Book Initiative; the Ontario Arts Council; the Canada Council for the Arts; and the Government of Canada, through the BPIDP, for our publishing activity.

Published in Canada by
Kids Can Press Ltd.
25 Dockside Drive
Toronto, ON M5A 0B5

Published in the U.S. by
Kids Can Press Ltd.
2250 Military Road
Tonawanda, NY 14150

www.kidscanpress.com

STANLEY CUP wordmark and image are registered trademarks of the NHL.
© NHL 2012 All rights reserved. Used with permission.

The artwork in this book was rendered in Adobe Illustrator.
The text is set in Providence-Sans Bold.

Edited by Yvette Ghione and Samantha Swenson
Designed by Per-Henrik Gürth and Julia Naimska

This book is smyth sewn casebound.
Manufactured in Buji, Shenzhen, China, in 3/2012 by WKT Company

CM 12 0 9 8 7 6 5 4 3 2 1

Library and Archives Canada Cataloguing in Publication

Gürth, Per-Henrik
    Canada in words / Per-Henrik Gürth.

ISBN 978-1-55453-710-5

1. Canada — Pictorial works — Juvenile literature.
2. Vocabulary — Juvenile literature. I. Title.

FC58.G875 2012   j971   C2011-908166-0

Kids Can Press is a /@rus™ Entertainment company